For Raymond,
brightest and best

Copyright © 1994 by Camilla Ashforth

First U.S. edition 1995
First published in Great Britain in 1994 by Walker Books Ltd., London.

Library of Congress Cataloging-in-Publication Data
Ashforth, Camilla.
Humphrey Thud / Camilla Ashforth.—1st U.S. ed.
"First published in Great Britain by Walker Books Ltd., London"—T.p. verso.
Summary: Horatio the rabbit does a magic trick that makes him disappear into his sock, but it
does not work with his friend Humphrey Thud the elephant.
ISBN 1-56402-538-1 (reinforced trade ed.)
[1. Elephants—Fiction. 2. Rabbits—Fiction. 3. Toys—Fiction. 4. Magic tricks—Fiction.] I. Title.
PZ7.A823Hu   1995
[E]—dc20            94-10449

2 4 6 8 10 9 7 5 3 1

Printed in Hong Kong

The pictures in this book were done in watercolor.

Candlewick Press
2067 Massachusetts Avenue
Cambridge, Massachusetts 02140

# HUMPHREY THUD

## Camilla Ashforth

**CANDLEWICK PRESS**
CAMBRIDGE, MASSACHUSETTS

Horatio had learned a disappearing trick.

"One,

two,

three . . .

Hoopla!" he called, and jumped
into his sock.
"Can I do that?" someone asked.

It was Humphrey Thud.

"It's easy," said Horatio. "You just say the magic word and jump into the sock. Let's show James."

James was beside his Useful Box,
wondering what to draw.
"Can we show you our magic trick?"
asked Horatio. "Humphrey can
disappear."

Humphrey charged toward the sock.
"Hoopla!" cried Horatio.

*THUD!*

"Have I disappeared?" Humphrey asked.

"Some of you has,"
said James.

"I must have said the wrong magic word," said Horatio.

James had an idea. "That sock's too small for an elephant," he said. "I have something bigger in my Useful Box."

James took out a scarf and gave it
to Horatio.
"One, two, three . . . Hoopla!"
Horatio called. He threw
the scarf over
Humphrey.

A lot of Humphrey didn't disappear.

"Maybe Humphrey's just too big,"
said James. "Why don't you make
his hat disappear instead?"

Humphrey took off his hat and
waited, while Horatio looked
for a place to hide it.

Horatio was gone for a while.
Humphrey felt tired.

He sat down.

By mistake he sat on his hat.

When Horatio came back, he
couldn't see the hat anywhere.
"It disappeared," he cried.

"Hooray!" shouted Humphrey.

James was worried. He hoped the
hat wasn't in his Useful Box.
He opened the lid and looked inside.

James rummaged in his Useful Box.
Humphrey waited.
"This is my best cow," James said.

Humphrey really missed his hat.

"Can I have my hat back now?"
he asked.

Oh dear, thought Horatio.

Horatio tried to think of a magic
word to bring back Humphrey's hat.

"Bee!

Button!

Bumble!

BOO!" he cried.

But Humphrey's hat didn't come back.

"James could lend you something like this," said Horatio. "Maybe."

But James had forgotten all about
Humphrey's hat and was sorting
out his Useful Things.

"Peppermints!" he said. "I've found
my peppermints."

Humphrey stood up and stretched
his trunk toward James.
"Could I have a peppermint?"
he asked. "I like peppermints."

"Peppermints!" cried Horatio. "That's
the magic word. Look, Humphrey's
hat came back!"

Humphrey put on his hat and
took Horatio for a ride.
James sat down to draw.

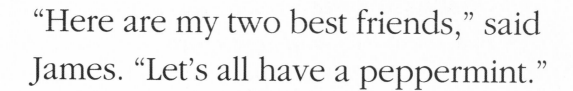

"Here are my two best friends," said
James. "Let's all have a peppermint."